Geoffrey Groundhog Predicts The Weather

BRUCE KOSCIELNIAK

Houghton Mifflin Company

Boston

For J. and P.

Copyright © 1995 by Bruce Koscielniak

All rights reserved. For information about permission to reproduce selections from this book, write to Permissions, Houghton Mifflin Company, 215 Park Avenue South, New York, New York 10003.

Library of Congress Cataloging-in-Publication Data

Koscielniak, Bruce.
Geoffrey Groundhog predicts the weather / by Bruce Koscielniak.
p.   cm.
Summary: When Geoffrey Groundhog pops out of his hole to predict the weather, he is blinded by television cameras and lights and is unable to see if he has a shadow. No one in town knows how to proceed, so Geoffrey needs help fast.
   RNF ISBN 0-395-70933-4 PAP ISBN 0-395-88398-9
   [1. Groundhog Day—Fiction. 2. Woodchuck—Fiction.]   I. Title.
PZ7.K8523Ge 1995   94-22426
[E]—dc20   CIP
                           AC

Printed in Singapore

TWP 20 19 18 17 16 15 14 13

One morning, after a long winter's nap, Geoffrey Groundhog popped out of his burrow to look for his shadow.
It was February 2, Groundhog Day.

Geoffrey remembered what his mother had told him.

"If you see your shadow on Groundhog Day, go back to sleep, because winter will last six more weeks.

"If there is no shadow, spring will soon be here."

Geoffrey hurried into town to tell the newspaper that he had not seen his shadow.

"So . . . no shadow, and spring is almost here. Is that it?" asked Merton Moose.

The story ran in that afternoon's *Daily Gazette*.

Groundhog Day Edition

The Daily Gazet

Serving all of

Vol. 15 – No. 35 – February 2

Groundhog Says no shadow Spring has Sprung!

By Merton Moose
Gazette Staff

Mooseflats County – Today at approximately 8:00 A.M. Geoffrey Groundhog popped out of his burrow and did not see his shadow. Geoffrey says the sky ry cloudy, and he ere but

Photo: M. Moose, Gazette staf

Spring into Warm Weat

Unpack spring cl and dust off golf e spring

Within a few days the weather turned warm, the snow melted, and the ground thawed. Spring had truly sprung! "Predicting the weather is easy," said Geoffrey.

The following winter, Geoffrey dozed snug as a bug, dreaming groundhog dreams in his warm nest at the bottom of his burrow.

Toward the end of January, folks started looking for clues as to what Geoffrey might predict.

As Groundhog Day drew near, television cameras and lights were moved into place around Geoffrey's burrow. This year, everyone would be able to watch the biggest, groundhoggiest Groundhog Day ever!

Bimble's TV Inc.
Spectacular Groundhog Day Sale
Big Big
One Week Only!
Super Groundhog EVENT
Rock bottom Prices
Groundhog Day Special
BIG
Local Groundhog TV Star
Geoffrey
able to watch
him on TV
on Groundhog
Day this
week. Will he see
his shadow
Super Brite Big Screen TV

Geoffrey's handsome picture had been popping up all over town.

17

Bright and early on Groundhog Day morning, everyone waited for Geoffrey.

One hour passed.

Two hours passed.

Three hours passed, yet still no Geoffrey.

"Geoffrey . . . hello Geoffrey!" called Merton. "Are you home?"

"Oh, no . . . I've overslept," groaned Geoffrey.

He flew out of bed,
dashed to his door . . .

. . . and made his appearance.

"Geoffrey, Geoffrey!" called Merton. "What did you see? Was there a shadow?"

"I don't know," cried Geoffrey. "With all the cameras and lights and everybody crowding around, I could hardly see the ground in front of me, much less my shadow!"

The Daily Gazette

Vol. 16 - No. 36   February 2   Serving all Mooseflats County

Groundhog Doesn't have a Clue

By Merton Moose
Daily Gazette

"I Don't know what I saw..." Says Geoffrey

Was there a shadow?

Weather Picture Muddled

Mooseflats – At 10:05 A.M. today Geoffrey Groundhog made his appearance and admitted he was foggy about whether he had seen his shadow.

Groundhog Daze

"I just can't say for sure what I saw," says Geoffrey.

Now things were really up in the air weatherwise. Nobody knew whether to bring out the golf clubs or the snow shovel. No one knew whether to wax the skis or the surfboard.

And no one had a clue whether to plug in the electric fan
or the electric blanket.

All weather reports were canceled.

"Geoffrey, this is causing major problems," muttered Merton. "We need your prediction now!"

"Ohhh, all right," moaned Geoffrey. "I'll have my answer by this afternoon."

EXTRA

Late Afternoon

The Daily Gazette

Special Groundhog Day Edition

VOL. 17 - No. 37

Geoffrey Says Winter six more weeks

It's Official... put springwear in mothballs

BY M. Moose

Mooseflats County - In an exclusive interview with the Gazette, Geoffrey Groundhog says the fog of doubt has lifted - it's six more weeks of winter. "No question about it!" says Geoffrey.

Gazette photo, M. Moose

Beyond the Shadow of A Doubt

Everyone was relie[ved] to hear that Geoffre[y] had made up his m[ind] [every]one will kn[ow]

"So Geoffrey, how could you predict that the winter will last six more weeks?" asked Rebecca Raccoon. "No one was really certain if there was a shadow or not. Did you guess?"

"Umm, no," said Geoffrey.

"Did you make a study of how weather works?" asked Sonny Squirrel.

"Nope," said Geoffrey. "To be honest, I called my mom. On Groundhog Day she always looks for her shadow, too!

"Whew," sighed Geoffrey. "Predicting the weather is very tiring. I'd better get back to my nest for a nap."

And that is exactly what he did.